Best Wishes, dear Maggie, [signature] 1/1/24

STORM GATHERERS

Crystal Valladares

PARTRIDGE

To order additional copies of this book, contact
Partridge India
000 800 10062 62
orders.india@partridgepublishing.com

www.partridgepublishing.com/india

CONTENTS

AUTHOR'S NOTE

Every story I write is set within my own experiences. In the case of Storm Gatherers, the setting is in a forest, ravaged by a storm. The convent school featured in this story, is similar to the one in a quaint village in Mangalore, South India, - a school which I often visited. The village sat at the edge of a dense forest and the monsoon always seemed fiercest here. The onslaught of rains that I experienced during my travels in South India was formidable to behold.

Children are naturally afraid of the fury of rainstorms. That was my inspiration.

Ensconced within the magic and mayhem is a unique story with an opportunity for self reflection.

I hope you will enjoy reading it as much as I enjoyed writing it.

Special thanks to my mother Dorothy Rodriguez and my son Joshua Valladares, who tirelessly read and evaluated initial drafts at least a hundred times. I also thank Damian Valladares for his invaluable advice, both legal and literary. And not forgetting my sister Meher Khanduja, for the image of her own home-made diya.

I am deeply grateful to Gennaro Evangelista for his unconditional support and complete faith in my literary prowess; to my brother Renato Rodriguez who allowed me to use his especially composed photographs; to ModBlackmoon Art for impressive creative efforts, and to the many friends and colleagues who spurred me on.

This story is for each of you – and to you, the reader. Enjoy it.

For Papa
Founder, J. J. Rodriguez Cours de Danse,
an institute of international repute

You were a star and you always will be

Trees huddled together like slaves being whipped by a cruel master

THE FIRST
ENCOUNTER

It was a stormy evening. Thunder crashed. Lightning ripped the clouds to shreds. Trees huddled together like slaves being whipped by a cruel master.

Twelve-year-old Namahh glanced up at the darkened sky through a thick network of trees. He had better hurry. He had an important task at hand. Picking the embroidered edge of his fine, hand-woven lungi[1], which hung until his ankles, he tucked it into his waistband so that it became knee length.

It was easier to move through the dense forest now, although he knew that his mother would not be pleased.

"A prince must always be properly dressed, no matter where he is," his mother had told him.

"But I am not a prince, Amma," said Namahh.

---

[1] A garment similar to a sarong, worn around the waist and extending until the ankles

1

"In this village you are," his mother said firmly. "Your father rules this village. Someday you will too."

Since then, Namahh was always careful about his appearance and ensured that his lungi hung down respectfully, until his ankles, like an elegant, white, embroidered sarong.

But things were different now. His father had been called to assist his cousin in a business matter and would not return home for several months.

"Handle things while I am gone," Namahh's father had told him as he climbed onto Raja, his favorite pure white stallion. "You're a good lad, Namahh. Take care of Amma."

"I will Appa," said Namahh. "I promise."

That was nearly a month ago.

The monsoon had set in now and Namahh's mother became gravely ill. The fever was high and although the special nursemaids kept her well hydrated, she was barely able to move.

"Hmmmmm," said the village doctor grimly, after examining Amma. He was a small man with a big smile and a moustache to match. His eyes twinkled with wisdom behind huge spectacles as he said, "The only remedy for Amma is the juice of the rare pink Karonda berry found deep in the forest."

"Hmmm," said the village doctor grimly

He peered at Namahh from above the rims of his spectacles, "But no one I know of has ever been able to find this rare berry, mind you."

"How do we know that this rare pink berry actually exists?" asked Namahh, worriedly.

"Well," said the village doctor walking out of the house with Namahh. "Sometimes exotic[2] birds drop partially eaten pieces of the rare fruit, so we know it exists. But no one has ever been able to find the tree that bore this sweet berry."

---

[2]   Nonnative

Namahh fidgeted nervously.

The doctor smiled kindly and said, "The pink berry certainly exists somewhere deep in the forest. Perhaps no one has found it yet, because of the impenetrable greenery.

The tree is probably hidden within clusters of other trees."

"The tree is probably hidden within clusters of other trees,"
said the doctor

Namahh thought about this for a long while and then made a decision.

"I will find the berries," Namahh announced later that day, to his surprised and anxious mother. "I promised Appa that I would take care of you."

Namahh set off the next morning

And without much fuss, he set off early the next morning, in search of this special fruit. He wore his father's red turban for good luck and slipped into a special, white long sleeved cotton kurta his mother had stitched for him weeks ago. "I will feel the presence of both Amma and Appa," he said to himself. "And I shall not be afraid."

Armed with a cloth bag for the fruit, and a small axe to cut stubborn foliage[3], Namahh carved a tiny path through the deep, dark jungle.

It was getting darker now, but Namahh was determined not to turn back until he had found the medicinal berries for his Amma.

When the rain started, it was already dusk. The canopy[4] of trees was so thick, that Namahh could not see the sky above him. He could only hear the rain as giant raindrops dripped onto him from the swishing leaves. But he could see nothing.

Then, quite suddenly, a dazzling white streak of lightning ripped through the trees in front of him, lighting up the forest for brief seconds.

A dazzling white streak of lightning ripped through the trees

---

3   vegetation
4   Shelter

With a loud crrrraaaack, branches crashed down, strewing the floor with fruits and flowers.

Namahh stood stock still, as fear raced down his spine. He sensed a fierce intensity[5] in the atmosphere around him.

There was a sizzle and sparks erupted as the air around him became charged with what seemed like electricity.

Thunder rumbled, low at first and then deafeningly loud.

Another branch cracked behind him as if someone had stepped on it.

Terrified, Namahh spun around. He saw nothing. Nearby, a smaller branch fell and Namahh felt the rush of plump fruit spill about his feet.

Immediately, the air was filled with a peculiarly[6] sweet aroma[7] of citrus and honey.

And there was something else. He felt a strong presence nearby, but he could see nothing in the darkness.

"Who is there?" asked Namahh, with as much courage as he could muster.

For a few tense filled moments Namahh heard nothing, but swishing trees and strong winds.

And then, he heard something – a whisper, soft and rustling.

---

5   Strength
6   unusually
7   perfume

"The storm is here."

Fear danced a jig[8] in his belly, but Namahh stood still as a rock. His mother always said that a true prince never allowed fear to get the better of him.

Suddenly, another thick stream of lightning sliced through the trees and touched the ground in front.

Namahh jumped back reflexively and stared in amazement at the way the light shone.

Namahh stared in amazement at the way the light shone

---

[8]   dance

The light froze like a spotlight in a theatre, and slowly encompassed[9] Namahh in its glow.

And then, the strangest thing happened. Glistening raindrops began to fall in a strange and magical pattern.

Glistening raindrops began to fall in a strange and magical pattern

---

9   surround

Within seconds a thin, white smoke arose from the ground and swirled around the mass of raindrops.

A thin white smoke arose from the ground

The watery mass took the shape of a woman, and the wisps of smoke slowly darkened and floated gracefully about her, like unending strands of hair.

Twigs and leaves attached themselves onto the woman

A sudden gust of wind lifted fallen twigs and leaves in a graceful arc, and they attached themselves onto the woman like clothes, giving her form and substance.

"The storm is here," she said again, in a voice that sounded as old as the Earth itself.

"But you need not be afraid," she murmured. "You are a good boy, Namahh. Your name says it all."

The image stared hard at Namahh. He stepped back fearfully.

"Do you know what your name means, boy?" she asked sternly. "We must always know what we are called."

Namahh stared, speechlessly.

"'Namahh' means to bow down to a higher power," said the lady slowly. "It is what you are always doing, whether you realize it or not."

She paused and then spoke again. "Look at how well you respected your father's wishes – taking care of your mother and other things."

"W-Who are you," stammered a frightened Namahh. "H-how do you know my name and so much about me?"

The strange apparition gave a little chuckle[10]. "We are Earth's Guardians," she said slowly. "We keep track of everything that happens on Earth."

Namahh stared wide-eyed, still afraid, but also curious.

"You will rule soon enough," continued the lady.

Suddenly aware of his untidily bundled up lungi, most unbecoming of a future ruler, he tried to hastily pull it down. But the lady floated up to him and he took an involuntary step back, nearly tripping in the process.

"Tell the people of Kudre that they must always protect their Earth," she said. "If people destroy what is good, then evil will reign. Shadow Creatures – ancient evil beings will rise from the depths of gloom and rule

---

[10]   giggle

Earth. They wait for opportunities to grow stronger. Do not give it to them."

Namahh shifted nervously, unsure of what to say.

The lady continued slowly, "If your Earth gets ill, people will fall sick too."

"My mother...," began Namahh, but the woman interrupted him. "We know," she said quietly. "Villagers have begun polluting the stream of clean water that flows past your house. Fish can't live in that water now. If it is not good for the fish, it is certainly not good for you." She peered[11] intently at him. "Your Amma used to drink water from that stream every morning. And now she is sick." Namahh hung his head in dismay.

"The storm will fill the stream with clean water again," the lady continued. "Keep it that way."

"Y-yes," muttered Namahh, determined to carry this message back to the people.

"The rain makes things right," she said, soothingly. "Haven't you heard the phrase, 'As right as rain?'"

Namahh nodded.

"Well hurry home now," said the lady briskly. "It is not safe for little boys to be alone in a dark, stormy forest."

"But I cannot do that," wailed Namahh, sadly. "I must find the rare Karonda berry for Amma. It is the only medicine that will cure her."

---

[11] Look closely

"But it is right here," said the strange woman. "Take it and she will be as right as rain!"

Namahh looked around incredulously[12].

"Where is it?" he asked. "I don't see it anywhere."

"Well we broke a branch and spilled the fruit, so that you could collect it easily."

"Look," she pointed at the ground. "The ground is full of it."

Sure enough, the ground was littered with strange, pink berries, the colour of a summer sunrise.

Namahh gave a gasp of joy and quickly picked as many as his cloth bag would hold.

Then he popped one into his mouth. Instantly the berry burst open, filling his mouth with the rich taste of citrus and sweet honey.

Delicious!

The woman smiled. "Earth has many precious gifts for you," she said. "You only need to take care of her."

Then she bent down and picked a fallen branch – a gnarled piece of wood from the Karonda tree.

"Take this," she said to Namahh. "It is special. Make sweet music out of it, and it will reveal the secrets of the forest to anyone willing to listen."

She thrust the branch into his hands and whispered into his ear, "Its music will cleanse the soul."

---

[12] Disbelievingly

Namahh stared at the old branch, wondering how he was going to get it to make any kind of music. He was about to ask her about it when the woman said briskly, "And now we must get you home."

Namahh was bundled in a cloud of sizzling energy

Before Namahh could react, he was bundled in a cold, cloudy fog of sizzling energy and whisked high up through the trees. His turban rolled off and a strong wind whipped at his hair. Although he could hear the heavy rain around, none of it touched him.

In a few minutes, he was gently placed down on a patch of wet grass, near his house.

The village was in darkness now, except for kerosene lamps burning in the windows of mud houses.

But Namahh was thrilled!

Not only did he have an important message for the people, but he also had the medicine for his mother.

"Ammmaaaaaaa..." he yelled loudly, as he raced towards home.

"Aaaammmaaaaaa, I have the berries. You are going to be as right as rain!

"Aaammaaaaaaa..."

Villagers poked their heads out of their houses to see what all the commotion was about.

"Namahh is back," they called out excitedly, from one house to another.

Within seconds, the whole village reverberated[13] with the good news!

"Namahh is back!"

---

[13] echoed

THE MAGIC OF KUDRE

Hidden within the dense folds of the deep green forest, was the tiny village of Kudre.

According to an ancient but popular folktale, the tiny village was once ruled by a powerful wizard named Vayu.

Vayu[14] was exactly like his name, always appearing like a breath of fresh air wherever he was needed. He was an extraordinary man with a long, flowing white beard and a big heart, always ready to help anyone in trouble.

---

[14] Breeze

Sometimes Vayu would tie his beard in a knot

His unusual beard had fine wisps of cloud infused[15] into it. Ages ago, when Vayu's grandfather, Namahh, was just a boy, he had had an encounter with the lightning and thunder during a rainstorm, deep in the forest. He spoke of 'Earth's Guardians,' - beings made up of the energy and elements of Earth. He spoke about rare herbs in the forest depths and he kept teaching people about the importance of protecting the environment.

Since then, every first born had some part of nature woven into them. And each child was named after some element of nature, to symbolize their oneness with Earth. Vayu's father Deep, whose name meant 'light,' had a fine sprinkling of sunshine, that hovered over his head like a halo[16]. Vayu's beard was streaked with thin strips of summer clouds. It constantly floated about him, as if it was being blown by a gentle breeze. Sometimes Vayu would tie his beard in a knot to keep it from flowing about too much.

On dusky evenings, villagers would gather under the thick old Banyan tree, for an evening of story-telling. Small round clay pots of hot, ginger tea were passed around, as the late evening sun bathed Kudre in a crimson glow. Vayu told grand tales about the strange beings made up of natural elements, that visited Earth during storms.

---

[15]   filled
[16]   circle of light

"Storm Gatherers," he said and paused dramatically, as he sipped his hot, ginger tea. "That's what my grandfather called Earth's Guardians."

He would pause and whisper gruffly, "But where there is good, there is also evil. My grandfather spoke about evil Shadow Creatures, who wait in the shadows, on the periphery[17] of our existence. They wait for an opportunity to capture our Earth and enslave us, if we allow them to."

The villagers listened in fascinated silence. Vayu would stroke his floating beard thoughtfully, take another sip of tea and continue in a quivering voice, "Greed, selfishness, cruelty, all of that gives evil the power to control us. Always let kindness rule your actions. That's why it is important to be good to our Earth. Take care of her. Be kind to her. Remember, Earth has her Guardians."

Then he would end the evening with music. It was the music that drew the villagers to these story telling sessions more than anything else. With a grand flourish, he would take out an old and ornately[18] carved flute. "My grandfather carved this flute himself from an old branch that he found deep in the forest," he told the villagers. Leaning forward, his eyes round and shining in the fading light, he would whisper to them hoarsely, "There is power within it. And its power touches the deepest part of the soul. Listen!"

---

[17] edge

[18] elaborately

He would put the flute to his lips and a hauntingly beautiful melody poured out of it. Soft and slow at first, it flowed forth in waves, reaching a crescendo[19] that promised great joy. The music evoked images of nature, beauty, happiness and all that was good. It struck a chord of deep harmony and peace within the listener. The wind carried these musical notes across the hills, and the valleys echoed with it. Anyone who heard this floating strain of music was immediately filled with gladness. Even after Vayu stopped playing, the notes vibrated within the natural surroundings. Night birds picked up the echoing strains and crickets acted as metronomes[20]. Within moments, Kudre had turned into a musical and magical place.

Vayu had no child to carry on after him, but he blessed the village with centuries of good times that he hoped would always surpass[21] the bad days. People believed that his magic, although not so powerful now, still worked to help villagers.

"His spirit flows with the wind," they said. "Through the breath of the breeze, he still showers us with eternal blessings."

---

[19]   climax

[20]   A device that produces a regular sound, like a clock, to help musicians play music at a certain speed

[21]   go beyond

When villagers could not explain certain occurrences, they said it was his "eternal good wishes" that caused problems to be solved so quickly. Things that were lost were soon found. Crops flourished despite bad weather. The people were good natured, and the village was a harmonious place to live in.

Sometimes, on cloudy nights, villagers returning home through the forest, would catch brief glimpses of a foggy white horse through the trees. It glided soundlessly, as if carried by the breeze. Almost immediately, a cool wind would bring snatches of a familiar, haunting melody. Villagers would strain to listen to it.

"It's Vayu's spirit," they would whisper. "He's letting us know that he still keeps watch over the village."

Villagers caught glimpses of a foggy, white horse that seemed to glide with the breeze

Now, over a century later, the younger generation of villagers laughed at these old stories their grandmothers told them.

They were still peace-loving people, but now the village was not as clean as it used to be. Trees were cut down, rivers were being polluted, and the wind often tossed littered garbage onto the street, to remind people about the good old days of cleanliness.

Still, on sunny days, Kudre was a picturesque little hamlet[22], surrounded by thick forests and dotted with pretty, red brick houses.

But tonight, it wasn't a pretty sight as stormy winds ripped it to shreds.

There was something fearful in the way the wind slapped its way through the trees.

---

[22] village

There was something fearful about the way the wind slapped its way through the trees

A large, fruit laden branch in the forest nearby crashed to the ground deafeningly. Streets became tiny rivulets of water as the rain pelted the earth. Families huddled together at home, drinking hot bowls of spicy lentil soup. Children hid themselves nervously, under bedsheets as they tried to fall asleep.

Not a soul dared to walk out on the dark streets

Rain drops as large as saucers hammered rooftops and not a soul dared to walk out on the dark streets. The village elders began to wonder about Vayu's words. Nature's fury is terrifying, he had told them. Our deeds, good or bad always boomerang right back to us.

But the youngsters of today did not believe in old fashioned legends. They cut trees as they pleased, preferred colored plastic bags instead of the handmade cloth bags their grandmothers stitched for them, and generally didn't care much for the Earth on which they lived. And now they were faced with nature's wrath. The village had never experienced a storm as fierce as this one.

"Nature's Guardians are furious," muttered the village headman Dhir, as he sipped hot soup and stared fearfully out into the night. "We have been destroying our Earth for too long now. The Storm Gatherers are here."

SISTER PIA

At the very end of the village of Kudre, hidden in a thick patch of greenery, was the old convent that housed the local school. In the old days it served as a Fort, but now much of it lay in ruins.

Photo credit Renato Rodriguez

The old convent school was once a Fort

A sudden burst of lightning lit up the sky and the school stood out against the horizon like an old abandoned castle, the turreted[23] roofs looming high.

It was an old grey stone structure, with long, shadow filled corridors and winding wooden stairways. Its cold walls, now scratched with time, looked like the thick leathery skin of a prehistoric beast. The ancient convent school sat like a fat old dragon in the middle of a two acre plot, on the edge of the forest.

With each deafening roar of thunder, the walls trembled and the stairways shook.

The windows along the long corridors glowed orange as candles flickered dimly.

Candles flickered dimly in the long corridor

---

[23]   Roofs built to look like small towers

At dusk, in the old days, people lit diyas to welcome blessings from the Almighty into their homes. Diyas were tiny clay pots with a cotton wick lying in a bed of specially made coconut oil.

In the old days people lit 'Diyas' at dusk

Now, years later, Sister Pia still continued the ancient Indian tradition. But in these modern times, the diyas were replaced with home-made candles that burned throughout the night.

Sister Pia hurried along the corridor replacing old candles with new ones

"Such a fearful storm," muttered Sister Pia to herself as she hurried along the long corridors, replacing old candles with new ones.

"I hope Trisa is alright."

She stopped in front of a small wooden door and slowly opened it. A tiny night lamp burned dimly. It was a child's bedroom and judging from the small bundle on the bed, Trisa appeared to be sound asleep.

Sister Pia waited a moment, in the doorway to Trisa's bedroom. Earlier that day, she had told the children at school about the old folktale. "According to the ancient legend[24], the fiercest rains brought with it 'Storm Gatherers' – magical beings that rode to Earth on giant raindrops," she said to her class of awe-struck sixth grade students.

"Although nobody had ever seen one, the village elders called these Storm Gatherers 'Guardians of the Earth.'"

The class had listened in fascinated silence, but Trisa raised her hand. She had a question.

"Why did the Storm Gatherers visit the Earth?" she wanted to know.

"Well," said Sister Pia, "People believed that these creatures often came down to Earth with a message for the people, usually about conservation. Sometimes, they chose special people to visit during the storm."

---

[24] Folktale

Sister Pia smiled as she pictured her class of intrigued students, and slowly closed the bedroom door.

Trisa was especially curious about the legend and at dinner time they spoke about it again.

"I hope it will not play on her mind, especially during this terrible storm," Sister Pia muttered to herself.

Sighing, she entered her own room. "Tonight is the perfect night for the Storm Gatherers," she said softly, as she closed her bedroom door.

TRISA

Another flash of lightning sprang out of the darkness, thin and crooked, like the gnarled hand of an old witch.

Thunder rumbled again.

Deep.

Low.

Menacing.

The windowpanes of the old convent rattled loudly, as if someone was trying to get in.

Shadows danced on the ceiling and in the corridors as candles flickered.

Trisa sat up in bed, terrified. Her petite twelve-year-old frame was hunched over her knees. Thick brown ringlets now bunched up in a ponytail, cascaded down to her shoulders.

Trisa sat up in bed terrified

Perhaps the raging storm had woken her up from her slumber.

Or was it something else?

Storms terrified Trisa. The sheer power of its uncontrolled fury was frightening.

Her tiny bedroom was cold and damp. Rivulets of rain ran down the closed bedroom window. It reminded Trisa of a million tears of grief running down a glassy cheek.

Trisa was an orphan. The nuns at the convent allowed her to study at the school, but she had chores to do in return.

She cleaned tables, washed windows, tidied cupboards, and helped other students with their school work.

Now, alone and frightened, she wondered if it was just the thunder that had woken her.

"Something is not quite right about the storm tonight," she said to herself.

But try as she might, she could not place what it was.

Trisa covered her ears, and shut her eyes tightly, trying not to think about the storm outside. But it was useless. She was terrified!

"I wonder if Sister Pia could really be sleeping through this fury of light and sound," she whispered.

Sister Pia was a study in severity

Sister Pia, or "Pious Pia" as she was secretly called, was one of the older nuns in the convent. She was a study in severity[25]. Thin, stern and straight, she was as sharp and precise as an arrow.

And just as lethal[26]!

She believed in following a path that was unforgivably straight and impossibly narrow. It seemed as if fun and frolic[27] were forbidden elements in her rigid[28] world of black and white. It was rumoured that Sister Pia feared nothing. Not even the devil himself.

But Sister Pia was kind to those who worked hard and prayed harder! Although at first glance she appeared grim[29], the children grew to love her stern ways and wry[30] humor. She was the one they wanted if they fell sick, or even if they simply had a nightmare!

Sister Pia had strict ways, undoubtedly, but beneath her strictness was a delightfully rare blend of comfort in times of distress.

Trisa had discovered that years ago, when she had first come to live in the convent, alone and frightened.

---

[25] strictness
[26] deadly
[27] Dance and skip
[28] stiff
[29] forbidding
[30] sarcastic

"Could Pious Pia really be sleeping through this raging storm?" wondered Trisa, aloud.

Perhaps not.

Perhaps she had been roused from her slumber too.

The other nuns were away on a special retreat – except for Sister Pia, of course. She had decided to pray in the solitude[31] of her quarters, while she took care of things at the convent.

Strange scratching sounds at her window roused Trisa from her reverie[32].

"screeeek, screeek, screeeeekkkk..."

What was that?!

A cold sliver[33] of fear did a cartwheel in her stomach.

Something was out there.

A coconut tree outside looked like the dark hand of a monster

---

[31] privacy

[32] dream

[33] slice

She looked at the rain splashed window. The distorted[34] image of a coconut tree outside, looked like the dark hand of an evil monster.

Trisa shivered at the thought.

A piercing squeal, thin and sharp, made Trisa sit up.

"Crreeeaaak..."

Despite the cacophony[35] of the storm, the whine filtered through.

"Crreeaaaakk..."

Trisa stared anxiously at the window.

What was that?

Perhaps it was a branch scraping the glass as the wind played with it.

"But there are no trees on this side of the convent - just a garden below, with a tiny play area," Trisa told herself.

Trisa strained her ears to listen, her heart beating wildly.

For a while she heard nothing but the rain beating furiously against her windowpane.

And then suddenly...

"Crreeeeekk.."

There it was again.

That whine sounded uncomfortably familiar.

Fear made her sweat, despite the chill.

And then she understood! The garden gate!

She now knew what that whine was!

---

34 Out of shape
35 noise

Trisa's eyes opened wide with anxiety that was steadily growing into full blown fear.

"It is the old wrought iron gate of the convent," she whispered to herself in shock. "That is the sound it makes when it swings open."

Trisa had locked the gates herself

The children played on it every day after school, much to Sister Pia's chagrin[36].

But there were no children there now.

"I locked those gates myself before the late evening prayer," said Trisa with a shudder of fear. "Who opened them?"

"Crreeeeaaak..." screeched the gate in protest, just as it did when the children played on it.

There was a momentary lull.

And then, again, "creeeaaak.."

Had the storm broken the lock and opened the gate? It sounded much too incredulous[37].

Panic-stricken, Trisa clutched her knees tightly to her chest.

Should she venture[38] to take a peek out of the window? She knew she should. Sister Pia and she were caretakers of this convent, after all.

She tried to move, but her legs wouldn't obey. Fear had bound them into a tight knot beneath her.

---

[36] annoyance

[37] unbelievable

[38] Dare to

MEJO

The peculiar scraping at her windowpane began again and she swung her head up in fear.

At first, she saw rivulets of water flowing down the windowpane

At first, she saw nothing but rivulets of water flowing down the windowpane.

But there was something odd about the way the water flowed. It seemed too thick – almost like dense sugar syrup.

"Calm down," Trisa told herself sternly. "It's just the heavy rain!"

She was about to look away, when something unusual caught her attention.

She drew a sharp breath and stared in shock, unable to move.

A most peculiar sight unfolded before her eyes.

Trisa watched intently, hypnotized by a mixture of fear and curiosity.

The streams of water on the pane outside began at first, a slow and unnatural movement. Droplets seemed to congeal[39], forming a thick, watery mass. Each drop rolled quickly towards the next, fusing together to form a shape. Swelling waves of water began to take on an unusual, but human form. From the thick puddle of water, a figure slowly arose.

---

[39]   thicken

From the thick puddle of water, a figure slowly arose.

Trisa continued to stare, now more fascinated than afraid.

The rising figure slowly grew larger. Features began to form. Within seconds, the water had shaped itself into the image of a little boy, crouching on the window ledge outside. He peered at her intently. Trisa instinctively drew back. The cherubic[40] face continued to stare, titling its head to one side for a better view, wide eyed and curious. It was a strange, translucent[41] face, made up of what looked like a million drops of water. The lips parted into a watery smile.

Trisa shrank back.

---

[40]   angelic

[41]   Semi-transparent

It could see her!

A new wave of fear swept through her and she shut her eyes tightly, hoping the image would disappear. Perhaps it was her imagination. It was not unusual for the mind to conjure up strange images in times of fear.

"screeekkk, screeekkk..."

The odd scratching at her window began. She looked reflexively towards it.

There it was again, the water creature.

But now, it held out a watery hand, beckoning[42] her toward the window.

It held out a watery hand against the windowpane

---

[42] gesturing

Trisa shook her head in horror.

"Never!" she hissed, frightened. "Go away!"

She just wanted to go back to bed and pretend that this was not happening. Certainly she was not going to venture by the window now!

"Go away," she hissed, frightened.

But then, a far more shocking thing happened.

From the corner of the window, where the frame was just the tiniest bit loose, a steady stream of water began to pour in.

Trisa stared, stunned, silently mouthing the word, "No!"

Trisa now faced a new storm within her - a storm of abject[43] terror. And it was much worse than the rainstorm outside.

She watched, horrified, as the face outside grew smaller and formless as it poured itself silently into her bedroom.

Fear propelled[44] her into action. She did a quick calculation and decided that she could run out her bedroom door in less than 10 seconds. It would take at least a minute to run down the dark corridor to Sister Pia's room, at the very end.

A most unpleasant exercise, no doubt, the kind that nightmares are made of. The corridor itself was filled with shadows and even during the day it was a cold and eerie place.

But Trisa had no time to ponder about the shadows in the corridor.

---

43   Absolutely hopeless, miserable
44   Forced

Her immediate task was to get away from a strange and very real watery horror. The bedroom door was just a few seconds away!

In a blink, Trisa threw off her bed covers, got off the bed, rushed towards the door...

..and crashed straight into a cold wall of water.

"Aaaagghhhh," she gasped loudly at the sudden shock of it and stood stock still in fear.

The wall of water slowly began to shape itself into the image of a little boy, just as tall as she was.

Trisa shrank back in fright. The water image gave her a smile and held out its watery hand. Tiny waves of water moved delicately along its torso with even the slightest movement.

"I am Mejo," said the image in a most peculiar, muffled tone, as if he was speaking underwater.

"Come with me," he said softly.

Trisa stepped back terrified. She opened her mouth to scream, but no sound came out. The butterflies in her stomach had metamorphosed[45] into gigantic[46] wasps and she turned white with fear.

The water boy drifted closer to her, leaving behind a trail of wet footprints.

---

[45] Transformed

[46] Huge

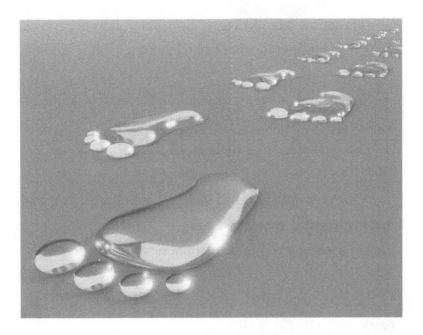

The water boy left a trail of wet footprints

"Do not be afraid," he droned calmly.

"We are here to show you something incredible. Chase away your fear of storms. You will learn some valuable lessons too."

He stared at her for a long moment and then added, "Come, ride the storm with me."

Trisa looked troubled and uncertain. Perhaps she was still asleep and this was an awful dream. She pinched herself hard to check if she was awake. She was!

Mejo looked at her with a twinkle in his eye.

"Perhaps you could learn a little about how to protect your environment too! Look at what is happening to your Earth."

Something in his manner knocked away some of Trisa's apprehension.

She swallowed and then spoke.

"I - I can't leave this place..."

"Oh you aren't leaving," said Mejo amused. "You are just visiting the outside for a bit.

Let me show you how to conquer your fear and truly ride a storm."

He gave her a sly wink, "Perhaps we can swing on the garden gate too!"

Trisa stared at him as realisation slowly dawned.

"So it was you, swinging on the garden gate then! But the lock..."

"...cannot keep the storm out," chuckled Mejo.

He extended his hand again.

"Now come, unlock those mental shackles[47] of fear and embrace the storm!

Learn something new. And teach others what you have learnt."

"B - But I would get drenched," countered Trisa as she lay back on the pillows, thinking about the possibilities.

---

[47]   Bonds

"B-but I would get drenched," countered Trisa
as she lay back against the pillows

Mejo smiled. "Not unless I want you to," he said in a watery murmur.

"Look!"

He pointed a finger at her and a tiny spray of water flew at her. She shut her eyes reflexively. He drew it back just before it touched her face.

"We are Storm Gatherers," he said proudly. "We are the water. No harm shall come to you, unless you ask for it. Come."

RIDING tHE STORM

Trisa stared at Mejo, her heart thumping. Excitement mixed with nervousness made her shuffle from one foot to another.

Storm Gatherers!

She had heard all about the ancient legend.

"The Storm Gatherers watch Earth at all times," Sister Pia had told Trisa earlier, at dinnertime. "When the time is right, they visit Earth."

Then she had smiled and added, "Who knows, perhaps one day you may run into one!"

And now, here she was, having a conversation with a magical being made up of storm energy!

Mejo presented her with a unique opportunity to conquer her fear of storms.

Should she take it? Surely she would return home, and be safely in bed well before daylight.

Mejo held out his hand and smiled gently.

Trisa made her decision.

She slowly put her hand into his.

It was the strangest experience. His hand felt smooth, cold and firm, like a transparent water mattress.

In one swift movement, Mejo heaved her over his shoulder and rose up into the air.

The window flew open and Trisa screamed as they glided out over the ledge, at lightning speed.

Grabbing Mejo tightly, she braced herself for the pelting rain and the slap of wind, but astonishingly[48], there was none. It felt as if she was racing through the air, in a cold, glass encased shell.

Mejo controlled the storm and she was untouched by it.

Around her, she could see the onslaught[49] of raging winds.

Rain slammed against roof tops. Trees bent low, swishing in the gale. Floods snaked through time-trodden trails, making the paths to the convent inaccessible.

---

[48] Surprisingly

[49] attack

"There's water everywhere," said Trisa

"There's water everywhere," said Trisa shocked to see the streets turn into small rivers. "People won't be able to walk there now."

"Well," said Mejo seriously. "Where there is a cause, there is an effect."

"What does that mean?" asked Trisa.

"Nothing happens without a cause or a reason," answered Mejo. "What you see now, is the result of selfishness, carelessness and greed. People have littered so much, that drains are clogged. Trees are cut down mercilessly, so the soil is loosened. And now you see the effect – floods."

Trisa listened quietly as Mejo continued to explain things. "People will soon destroy Earth if they do not change their ways. And then, when goodness is destroyed, evil takes over. People will forget the concept of love and compassion. That would be disastrous for the living. Why can't people be more compassionate? Why can't they love nature? They will only be rewarded if they do. Nature has immense treasures to offer. And she shares every one of them."

They rode in silence for a moment. Then Mejo spoke again. "We Storm Gatherers unleash the fury of storms so that people understand that Earth needs to be respected. We also cleanse the Earth."

They flew in what felt like an arc, rising high towards the darkened sky and then racing down toward the rain shattered Earth again. Over rolling hills and dales, they glided, as the lightning lit up the Earth.

Photo credited Renato Rodriguez

Over rolling hills and dales they glided

After a while, Mejo flew down to a wooded area.

"Look there," he said, pointing to a dark area below them. Sure enough, in a hidden corner of the forest, amid a pile of cut down tree limbs, was a huge heap of garbage. Plastic bags dripped like sodden, filthy rags. A pool of dirty water collected at the base of the pile and spilt onto the paths leading to the streets.

Trisa gasped, shocked and disgusted.

"There is your answer," said Mejo. "That is the reason for the floods. When the villagers see these floods they will get the message about caring for their Earth."

Trisa quietly made up her mind never to litter again. She decided to tell her classmates too about the dangers of littering.

"You are right, Mejo," said Trisa softly. "We need to change the way we are. We must be the change."

Mejo smiled.

"Indeed you are a special girl, Trisa. No wonder I was sent to visit you!"

Trisa could not help feeling a little thrilled when he said that. She was the chosen one!

SILvER LINING

A nd then they rose again, higher than ever before. The Earth shrank into a myriad[50] dull colours, but the sky seemed alive and palpable[51] - a maestro[52] clad in a heavy, two-toned purple cloak, orchestrating a clear balance of storm music.

"The storm paints the heavens in shimmering shades," said Mejo. "Look!"

They were far above Earth now, flying through the clouds.

Trisa stared at swirling cloudy mists all around her. Everywhere she looked, cloudy masses churned, turning into spectacular shades of purple and turquoise, interspersed with splashes of silver.

It was breathtakingly beautiful.

---

[50] countless
[51] Touchable or solid
[52] Person who conducts an orchestra

They flew towards a thick, foamy piece of steel grey cloud and Mejo heaved himself onto it. He placed Trisa down by his side. Instantly, she sank into what felt like a soft, downy mattress. She gave a little squeal of surprise.

"We are sitting on a cloud!" she exclaimed delightedly. She leaned over the edge for a breath-taking view of the Earth.

Trisa leaned over the edge of the cloud for a breath-taking view of the Earth

"Well it is a night of magic," laughed Mejo, "And there's much that I want you to see."

He pointed out into the distance.

"Look," he said. "Those are thick, dark clouds, but they are beautiful too. Do you know why?"

Trisa stared at the clouds in the distance. They looked like thick, dark, twisting bits of smoke. But as they tossed about, the edges sparkled.

"They may be dark clouds, but they still shine," said Trisa, amazed at how beautiful it was.

"Every dark cloud has a rich silver lining," explained Mejo, pointing to the moving mass of clouds.

Every dark cloud has a silver lining

The cloudy mists swirled around them, like tufts of cotton silk. Sure enough, each cloud was edged with a streak of silver. It reminded Trisa of the silver embroidery on her birthday dress packed away in her wardrobe at the convent.

It was so beautiful, that Trisa could not resist reaching out and grabbing a stray piece of silver lined, purple cloud that floated close by her. It felt like velvet.

"Come along," said Mejo heaving her onto his back again. "There's more to see."

They leapt off the shimmering grey cloud and glided past other colourful cloudy masses.

"This is simply beautiful, Mejo," said Trisa, leaning down to talk to him. "I did not realise that storms could be so beautiful."

"Even these dark clouds have their own special beauty." She reached out and plucked another floating piece of turquoise cloud with a thick lining of silver.

"This silver lining is what makes it so."

The cloudy strand twisted gracefully in Trisa's hand. To her delight, it swirled around her neck like a royal, silver edged fur collar, before the wind pulled it away.

Mejo smiled and said, "The Earth is beautiful too. Look!" Then Mejo flew back down towards the Earth, at a tremendous speed. Trisa's hair streamed behind her as the wind whistled in her ears.

They were in the deepest part of the forest now – a place of untouched beauty. People couldn't reach this part of the forest because the dense foliage made it inaccessible[53]. It was the most beautiful place that Trisa had ever seen.

---

[53] unreachable

They flew over a tiny stream that babbled musically. The water twisted and turned like liquid silver and a family of yellow frogs sang in chorus on a large lotus leaf. Nearby, on a fallen tree trunk, a group of turtles stood in a row, enjoying the rain. Colourful reeds swayed gracefully like dancers. A tiny bright red fish jumped up in delight and dived back into the swirling waters again. Raindrops glistened on every grassy blade, like tiny fairy lamps.

A group of turtles stood in a row enjoying the rain

The sight was so enchantingly beautiful that Trisa gasped in happy surprise.

"This is such a happy place!" said Trisa clapping her hands in delight.

"It's clean too!" laughed Mejo, "Quite untouched by humans."

Suddenly thunder crashed deafeningly. Trisa jumped in fright and almost lost her balance.

"Whoa, there!" yelled Mejo, trying to steady himself. "Be still. Learn to enjoy that calm, even during a storm!"

Trisa held on firmly and closed her eyes, allowing her senses to soak in the pulsating[54] energy around her. She felt at peace.

Mejo craned his head to speak to her.

"When Earth gets too dark, grandma shines her torch like a beacon. You call it lightning.

And when grandpa sees the intense drama of the storm played out on Earth, he claps. That's why it is called a 'Thunderclap'.

It's nothing to be afraid of."

Trisa listened, fascinated.

---

[54] lively

wHen Darkness Comes

Just as Mejo said, a brilliant light flashed down from the heavens, lighting up the Earth for a moment. The effect was awe-inspiring. Everything the rain touched glittered. Paths now filled with water became tiny, shimmering streams. Leaves turned silver. Earth sparkled.

Earth sparkled

There was nothing sinister[55] about it. The beauty was breathtaking. Trisa wondered why she should have been so afraid of storms. There was so much beauty and so much to learn from it. She was about to tell Mejo that she was no longer afraid, when suddenly the Earth grew dark again. She could only hear rain drops and the rustle of the trees. But she could see nothing. Even the frogs had stopped their singing abruptly. The lightning was sucked up by thick, dark clouds and the heavens became a swirling haze of deep purple. The silver lining still shone on each cloud, but Trisa was more concerned with this terrible darkness now.

And then, in the darkness, something white shifted between the trees. What was that? She tried to peer harder between the trees, but she saw nothing. Fear gripped her and she held onto Mejo tightly. "It's suddenly so dark," Trisa whispered into Mejo's ear. "Where did the lightning go? Everything looked so beautiful in the light."

Mejo smiled quietly as he flew to a large old Pipal tree and gently placed her down on a broad branch, under thick foliage.

"It is always darkest just before you see the brightest light," said Mejo, perching himself besides her. "If you know that, then you will never be afraid of the darkness again. It is the darkness that makes the light so valuable."

---

[55] Evil

Trisa listened in silence, pondering about this new piece of information. Could that be true, she wondered, as she held on tightly to the thick, wet branch. "It is true," said Mejo, reading her thoughts. "You'll see."

Trisa's thoughts were interrupted by the sound of movement just ahead. She tried to look between the thick cluster of trees, into the blackness beyond. Suddenly very afraid, she clutched Mejo tightly and then she saw it again – a brief glimpse of something white rushing past, between the trees.

"Mejo," she whispered, frightened. "There's something out there. Look!"

"Do not be afraid of them," said Mejo soothingly.

"Them?" asked Trisa worriedly. "I thought that this part of the forest was impenetrable[56] - that there were no humans here."

"Not humans," whispered Mejo gently, "Spirits."

Trisa stared at him disbelievingly. Was he joking?

She saw that he was quite serious, so she asked anxiously, "You mean ghosts?"

"I prefer to call them spirits," answered Mejo. "They are simply living orbs[57] of energy that take on different forms. There are many spirits that protect Earth. Perhaps that is one of them."

---

[56] Dense

[57] Globes or circles

He paused a moment and then added, "We'll find out soon enough."

The movement on the ground below began again and Trisa looked in the direction of the sound. She couldn't see anything, but Mejo quietly pointed into the distance straight ahead of them.

"Look," he said in a soft whisper. Trisa strained to see what he was pointing at and then, quite suddenly, she saw it – a horse, so white that it looked transparent. It glided through the trees, almost as if it was carried forth by the breeze. It stood still for an instant, nibbling at the grass and then it turned its head and seemed to look directly up at them.

It stood still for an instant, nibbling at the grass

"It's a wild horse," said Trisa in awe. "And it is beautiful."

"An ancient spirit," said Mejo softly. "He knows this place.

And he knows you."

The horse bowed its head for an instant and in a swift blur, it shimmered and disappeared.

"Where did it go?" asked Trisa in amazement. "It seemed to disappear into the air."

Mejo smiled, reached across and pulled the supple, fruit laden branches of another tree toward him. A delicious citrus and honey aroma filled the air as a few ripe berries tumbled down. Mejo plucked a few of the sweet berries, offered them to Trisa and said, "The last time people tasted these berries, was centuries ago. Namahh was your age when he came looking for these berries to cure his sick mother."

Trisa listened in astonishment. She popped a berry into her mouth and tasted the sweetest explosion of lemon and honey.

"Namahh was a good boy," continued Mejo, "A great leader too. Your village prospered under him and his descendants. Vayu was one of them. His spirit looks after the forest."

They sat in silence for a while and then Mejo said quietly. "But things have changed now. The village is not what it used to be. People have become selfish and uncaring."

Then he looked at her and smiled. "But you are different, Trisa. You care, and so the universe will always care for you."

Trisa smiled, ate another berry and looked around at the impenetrable darkness.

"This darkness is just a passing phase," said Mejo, following her gaze. "Whenever we face a dark moment, the trick is not to be afraid. Just hold on and know that every dark moment is closely followed by a new and brilliant light. You just got to wait for it."

Trisa listened quietly, as Mejo continued to explain what he meant. "Life is filled with bright moments," said Mejo softly. "But sadly, many choose to dwell only on those few dark seconds in-between the good times. And when the light comes, they are so busy grumbling about the dark times, that they forget to enjoy the light." Mejo paused to take a breath and added, "Such grumblers are doomed to live in darkness forever, because they have forgotten to appreciate the light. But the light does come, far sooner than you think."

Trisa thought about this as she stared out into the blackness and a deep-rooted pain suddenly surfaced. She had faced many dark and unhappy moments too.

But then, her thoughts were interrupted by soft strains of the strangest, but most beautiful music she had ever heard. "Someone is playing the flute," she whispered, "Who could that be?"

"Shhh," said Mejo, "You are about to receive an invaluable gift."

"A gift?" asked Trisa in surprise. "What gift? From who?"

Mejo whispered softly into her ear, "The gift of freedom."

Trisa stared at him questioningly, as Mejo continued, "The forest shares its secrets with you. There is power in it. Allow yourself to listen and learn."

Soft strains of music floated up to them as Mejo spoke again, "The music seeks to cleanse your soul of all pain. Surrender to it. And be free."

Trisa did not quite understand what he meant, but she stayed quiet.

The music was soothing. Trisa closed her eyes and listened to the peace-filled notes. It tugged at her heart, forcing her to address and release the pain that was buried deep within - a pain that she had hidden from her conscious mind, but which festered, deep within her soul. The notes guided her thoughts, unleashing a flood of long-lost memories – memories of deep sadness and great joy. As she listened to the quiet rhythm of the flute, she felt her eyes sting with tears of joy and sadness – of darkness and light.

Spellbound by the mesmerizing[58] lilt[59], her thoughts flowed with the music, taking her back in time to the

---

[58] hypnotic

[59] tone

heart wrenching memories of her darkest days, when she was first sent to live in the convent.

She was just a baby then, an orphan that no one wanted. People said her mother had passed away soon after she was born, and no one knew where her father was. All she had to remind her of her parents, was a thin gold chain with a tiny locket in the shape of a heart. Within it was a photograph of her parents on their wedding day.

The haunting music became stronger and slowly started to peak. Old forgotten memories resurfaced and Trisa was taken back in time, to her first day at school. Sister Pia had taken her to meet the assistant head mistress, Janina Kurr, an overbearing, outspoken heap of a woman, clad in a long, shapeless kurti that made her large, towering frame look even larger. "We can't keep this thing at our school," she boomed loudly, wrinkling her nose in disgust at little Trisa, as if she was looking at a small pile of garbage.

The music in the forest reached a crescendo, as Trisa relived the fear she felt all those years ago. Janina Kurr's nasty voice terrified little Trisa and she sank down to her knees, cowering in fright, hugging onto her ragged old teddy bear. Peering fiercely at Trisa from above her horn-rimmed spectacles, Miss Kurr added rudely, "Take her to an orphanage."

Trisa sank down to her knees, cowering in fright

Recalling those dark and terrible moments, Trisa now felt hot tears stream down her cheeks. She remembered running to Sister Pia, and crying into the folds of her skirt, terrified. That was the darkest time of her life, but it was over now.

The music turned soft. Melodious notes floated forth, and she felt soothed.

Trisa sighed deeply and as she exhaled, every unhappy thought that was buried deep within, left her mind. She felt cleansed.

Now a different strain of music filled the air. Low and hypnotic, the music evoked feelings of hope and happiness. It took Trisa back to that old school office, but now she felt the comforting touch of Sister Pia as she buried her face into her skirt. Janina Kurr may be a giant bully, but Sister Pia was Head Mistress, formidable[60] in her own way and quite the opposite of her assistant. Stern and dignified, with a quiet strength that belied[61] her slim stature, she was not one to be trifled[62] with.

---

[60] tough, fearsome

[61] contradicted

[62] toyed with

Sister Pia aimed her words at Janina Kurr, "Trisa stays here."

Straight as an arrow, she aimed her words at Janina Kurr - slow, deliberate and sharp, in a manner that left no room for argument. "Trisa stays here."

And since then, nothing was the same again.

The lilting strains of the flute shifted again. It rekindled the happiness that Trisa felt at that moment of triumph. She smiled at the thought of it. Janina Kurr had looked away uncomfortably, her fat double chins turning triple, as she looked down at her cluttered desk. But Trisa's world had brightened instantly. The nuns doted over her and her friends at school made her forget her troubles. The light of happiness had chased away her darkness.

The unearthly music turned soft and slowly faded into the patter of raindrops. Trisa breathed deeply. A burden had been lifted. She felt free.

Far away, between the cluster of trees, a shimmering white image of an old man with a long, flowing beard glowed dimly. He held a flute lightly to his lips, but he had stopped playing now. Yet, the forest was alive with the vibrations of his melody.

Then he turned and looked up at her. A hint of a smile played on his lips. In the darkness, Trisa smiled back and she felt a strange connection with this ancient soul. The wind shifted, and the apparition melted into a fading image of a foggy wild horse.

Trisa couldn't stop looking at the image before her, but she wasn't afraid now. "It's Vayu, the flute player," she said softly to herself, "The guardian of the forest."

She continued to stare in awe at the last wisps of the fading apparition and she whispered, "Thank you."

Mejo's voice brought her back to the present moment. "Do you understand now?" he asked, peering at her intently. "You were deep in thought."

"Yes, I do," whispered Trisa. "Indeed, the light does come. We are never in the dark for long." She paused for a moment and then added gratefully, "Thank you for making me realize that."

As soon as she uttered those words, a thick stream of lightning flashed down, turning everything silver.

The world lit up, as bright as day!

Mejo smiled at her and jumped up. He heaved Trisa onto his back in one smooth movement. "Come along," he said quickly. "The light is here!"

He shot upwards through the trees and Trisa gasped in delight at the scene before her. She leaned down, straining to look through the branches of the tall trees as Mejo flew higher. The village of Kudre shimmered brightly, like a magical place, straight out of a fairytale. Bright colored mushrooms sat in clusters at the foot of tall trees and shining insects flitted about and played among them.

The village of Kudre shimmered brightly

They sailed past an owl's nest in the hollow of an old tree. The owl popped her head out of the hollow and hooted at them in surprise. Trisa laughed as they whizzed past. They brushed past a blossom filled branch and the nest of a sleeping sparrow. "Tweeeet," chirped the sparrow, mildly annoyed at being disturbed. She spread her wings over her sleeping babies protectively and nodded off to sleep again. "Sorry," whispered Trisa to the sleeping sparrow family. The world was beautiful. Even more so than before! Everything seemed brighter now as each raindrop reflected the power and the beauty of light.

THE STAIRWAY TO HAPPINESS

A nd then a strange thing happened.
The lightning flashed and froze into a tight beam
of light, aimed directly at Mejo and Trisa.

The lightning flashed and froze into a beam of light

Trisa blinked in the glare shielding her eyes, but Mejo gave a squeak of excitement.

"What did I tell you about a bright moment always following the darkest one?" said Mejo excitedly.

"You are going to have a brilliant surprise, Trisa!"

Trisa smiled down at him, confused.

"What brilliant surprise?" asked Trisa. "I just saw the world lit up and it was simply splendid!"

"Well here's something even more splendid," replied Mejo.

"It's grandma!

She's inviting us into the heavenly realm!

Look!"

The shining white beam of light shimmered for an instant, and then transformed into a most unusual stairway, leading high up into the clouds.

The stairway shone like a million stars

Mejo pointed at the glittering white flight of stairs that descended toward them. It shone like a million stars.

"Not everyone embraces storms as you chose to do," said Mejo, as he glided gracefully towards the glowing stairway. "People are afraid to let go of their fears. They allow fear to control them."

Then he turned and smiled at her, "But not you! You are a brave one. And now grandma wants to reward you."

"Come," he said, as he gently placed her down at the foot of the stairway.

Trisa stood on the first step of the gleaming stairway and looked around in amazement. It was the most beautiful sight she had ever seen. The stairway shimmered and shone, as if it was carved out of a giant diamond. Trisa felt a surge[63] of happiness.

"That is the Stairway to Happiness," said Mejo softly. "Very few have been lucky enough to be invited to ascend it. But it is not an easy climb to the top. It takes strength, determination and courage."

Trisa listened, spellbound.

"It is beautiful, isn't it?" asked Mejo.

"It is," whispered Trisa. "But why is it called the Stairway to Happiness?"

---

[63] Gush

"The Stairway to Happiness leads you to success. When you reach the top, it means that you have achieved your goal. Achievement brings happiness."

Mejo paused and added, "And your goal right now is to meet grandma. She knows how special you are."

Trisa smiled, but Mejo turned serious.

"As always, the climb to the top is a difficult one," he said.

"Night creatures who sit in the shadows will try to lure you away"

"Night creatures who sit in the shadows of the stairway will try and distract you or lure you into the dungeon of the damned. Don't let them bring you down."

Mejo craned his watery head and peered deeply into her eyes.

"The Shadow Creatures can take any shape. They are deceptive creatures."

The shadow creatures can take any shape or form

"Do not get waylaid[64] by them, or you will be trapped in a dark world that hovers[65] between the time zones of the past and the present."

He added solemnly[66], "And you will be lost in a nightmare, forever."

---

[64]   Trapped by

[65]   Drifts

[66]   Seriously

THE CLIMB TO THE TOP

Trisa listened, her fascination laced with fear.

"Focus on your goal to reach the top. Don't let anyone drag you down, - unless of course something important requires your attention."

Mejo waited, in case she had a question.

She did not, so he continued. "You must use your judgement. Often we are so focused on reaching our goal that we don't care or notice who we trample on in the process. And that is an important choice – to achieve quickly what we want, or to let kindness guide the path to success."

There was a moment of indecisiveness[67] as Trisa nervously wrung her hands.

But then Mejo smiled his watery smile at her and she relaxed a little.

---

[67] Uncertainty

"You're a smart girl - and a kind one too. You'll know what to do. Just stay focused and move ahead".

And with that, he leapt far ahead, onto the glittering stairway.

Trisa watched him go, feeling suddenly very alone.

But then he turned and glided back to Trisa, as if he had forgotten to mention something.

"Whatever you do, do not step outside the perimeter of light. If you do, it will be difficult to get back on track. Don't let darkness pull you out of the light. Always move forward, toward the light."

"Wait," said Trisa anxiously. "Let's climb to the top together. How will I manage alone?"

Mejo smiled apologetically, "I cannot accompany you unfortunately. The climb to the top is always done alone. We can only advise you on how to reach there."

He stared at her for a brief moment and said, "Do not let fear hold you back. You have come so far already."

He gave her a quick wave and was gone.

Trisa was left behind, alone, blinking in the brightness. She could see Mejo far ahead, almost invisible in the brilliant glare.

She had a terrible urge to call him back to be with her for a bit longer. He was still within earshot. The temptation almost got the better of her, but she scolded herself in time. She was a brave and courageous girl. She could do this.

It looked like a peaceful climb to the top

Alone on the stairway, Trisa took a moment to soak in the quiet beauty around her. The stairway seemed to be carved out of the purest crystal - smooth and dazzling. It looked like a serene[68] climb to the top. Some of her apprehension[69] melted away.

A dark fog hovered at the far edges of the stairway and Trisa felt nervous just looking at it.

"Focus!" said Trisa sternly to herself as she turned away and began her ascent.

As she placed her foot on each step, it glowed brighter for an instant. The steps looked slippery as they shimmered, but when she stepped on each one, it felt firm and steady.

She felt reassured.

---

[68] Peaceful

[69] Uneasiness

SHADOW CREATURES

As soon as Trisa started to ascend the stairway, a small dark face appeared from the surrounding shadows.

"Please," it whimpered in a high-pitched squeal. "Help me, I'm stuck."

Trisa hesitated. Mejo had told her not to get distracted.

She tried to look at the edges, beyond the brightness, but she could see only smoky fog. The stairway gleamed brilliantly before her and she started to ascend it again.

She had barely climbed a few stairs, when she was interrupted once more.

"Please," said the dark face again.

Strange disembodied voices seemed to be coming at her

There was whispering and shuffling and then an agonised moan from the foggy edges of the stairway.

Trisa stopped and looked around.

Strange, disembodied[70] voices seemed to be coming at her from both sides of the stairway. Tiny faces appeared to peer at her from the dark perimeter. But when she tried to look at them, they immediately shrank back.

---

[70] Ghostly

"If you would just step on to the edge of the stairway, you could help me," said a small dark shadowy image that Trisa could hardly see.

"Where are you," asked Trisa, peering into the foggy edge.

She squinted in the glare and stared intently in the direction of the speaker, but she saw nothing – just a rolling black fog at the very edge.

She waited a moment, but no one spoke again. So Trisa took another step up.

And another.

She was about to place her foot on the next step when a tiny voice whispered, "Why won't you help us?"

Trisa turned to look at the face that seemed to talk to her, but it immediately receded into the shadows. All she heard was a harsh and urgent whisper, "Please!"

The face receded into the background

"How can I help?" asked Trisa, feeling concerned.

Once more, she strained to look, but the brightness made it difficult to see what lay at the edges of the flight of stairs.

"Who are you?" she asked. "And where are you trapped?"

No one answered her.

Trisa suddenly felt undecided. Should she continue on her journey up or should she stop and investigate?

She waited a moment, looking around anxiously. Everything turned quiet again.

She took another step up...

...and was interrupted again by the small, high-pitched voice. "Please! I'm right here at the very edge. Help me."

Trisa stopped and stared in the direction of the voice, feeling a combination of fear and concern. Then, out of the darkness, a face appeared. Trisa gasped in shock at its sudden appearance.

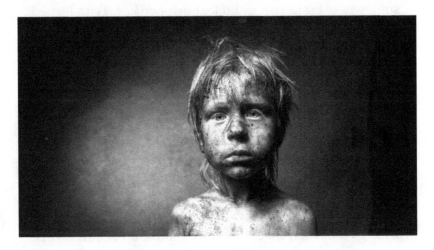

It was a little boy, dirty and unkempt

It was a little boy, dirty and unkempt. Wordlessly, he pointed at the darkness behind him.

Trisa tried to follow his gaze but she saw nothing.

"Little boy," began Trisa, "Who are you? Are you lost?"

The child stared at her mournfully for a moment. Then he turned and walked purposefully into the darkness.

Trisa hurried after him. "Stop! Let me help you."

She rushed after the child, concerned that he may be hurt. But the closer she got, the further away he seemed to disappear into the black fog.

"Wait," Trisa called out after him.

But the little boy had vanished. Trisa stood helplessly near the edge of the circle of light, wondering what to do.

There were shuffling sounds from the dark fog and agitated whispering. She heard a little boy cry out from somewhere far beyond, and fear gripped her. Trisa leaned forward cautiously and tried to peer into the darkness.

But she saw nothing.

Perhaps someone was in trouble and needed her assistance. She remembered Mejo's advice about the rise to the top. Was it important to achieve her goal right now, or should she delay it for a bit so that she could help someone who needed her?

She stood, undecided and anxious, wondering about what to do, when the shrill voices spoke up again. "We're here," thin voices urged her on. "A little more towards the edge..."

Trisa considered her options. "I could go quickly to the edge and do my best to help whoever is in trouble," she told herself. "It will only take a few minutes. And then I can resume my climb to the top."

A piercing scream made her jump. "You need to come to the edge," yelled a shrill voice. "We need you here."

"Where exactly are you," asked Trisa, her eyes wide with concern.

"We're here!" several voices cried together. "In the Pit of Gloom."

Trisa made her decision.

ON THE BRINK
OF DARKNESS

Trisa took tentative[71] steps towards where the step broke off sharply into the blackness, at the very end of the glittering stairway.

As she moved away from the dazzling stairs, her path grew dimmer.

The cries of agony grew louder as she approached, and she quickened her pace. She wondered who was trapped out there in the dark, and how they got there.

Trisa was so intent on trying to help, that she walked just out of the area that the light touched. Without realising it, Trisa had left the light behind her.

---

[71] Cautious

"Where are you?" she called out anxiously in the sphere of darkness.

As soon as she entered the dark zone, a horrible uneasiness gripped her.

When she reached the dark perimeter, all movement seemed to have frozen. It was like a soundless vacuum.

She looked around fearfully. "What is this place?" she whispered to herself anxiously. "There are others here. I can sense it. But I can see nothing."

Taking a deep breath, she called out again, "Hello? Is anybody there?"

No one answered her.

There was an air of meanness and deceit. She had an uncontrollable urge to turn around and run back, but she did not. She was here to help. And she would do just that.

"Where are you," she called out anxiously as she stepped into the sphere of darkness.

She was surprised to hear her voice, so high-pitched and frightened.

Clearing her throat, she added a little more courageously, "I don't see anyone."

An icy breeze wrapped itself around her and she shivered. "Little boy," said Trisa nervously, "I am here to help. Where are you?"

The sudden silence was terrifying.

From the distance just ahead, she could feel the pull of negative energy, like a sordid invitation into a pit of gloom. And it seemed to reek of all that was evil.

The impenetrable blackness was deep and consuming. Trisa felt a wave of dizziness. "What is this terrible place," she whispered again, as she tried to steady herself.

She tried to take a step back.

She could not.

Her legs would not move. She was at the very edge of the stairway and no light touched the edge, except for a dull, backlit glow. She was trapped.

Frightened, she turned to look behind her and saw that the light was just an inch or two away.

Mejo had told her not to leave the perimeter of light, but she had.

"What have I done," said Trisa in dismay. "I must get back into the light."

She had barely spoken, when a child's voice said, "I'm here!"

Before Trisa could react, the little boy loomed up in front of her, grinning crookedly. "Welcome," he said, grabbing her hand and pulling her forward, "...into the Pit of Gloom."

THE PIT OF GLOOM

P anic-stricken, Trisa struggled to free herself, but the boy had a fierce grip. In a second, Trisa was enveloped in a cloud of blackness. She was now deeper inside the dark zone. "Who are you?" she screamed, terrified of the boy now.

The boy released her and moved away. His features slowly began to change into a dragon-like creature. "We are Shadow Creatures," he said, in a voice that sounded ancient. "We capture those who enjoy darkness, destruction and greed. They become our slaves." As he spoke, his features changed again.

Trisa stared, horrified.

"W- where am I?" she asked, shivering with cold and fear.

The boy's features melted and reappeared again as an old witch. "Oh, you are in the Pit of Gloom," she cackled in amusement. "This place has been created and strengthened by the wickedness of people," she droned. "It is what happens when one loses the ability to love."

With an evil chuckle, the old witch disintegrated into a pile of dust.

Trisa stared in shock.

Within seconds, the dust began to rise and take the shape of a large wolf. Sparks flew out of its mouth as it spoke. "When people on Earth become selfish, we become stronger." It barred its teeth at her and growled, "One day we shall rule Earth."

Then it disappeared into thick black smoke, only to reappear again as a hooded old man.

Pointing a gnarled hand at her he said, "We also take those who surrender to panic."

Pointing a gnarled[72] hand at her he spoke in a deep voice, "We also take those who surrender to panic."

Then he smiled wickedly and added, "We feed on fear."

He took an unsteady step toward her and spoke in a threatening whisper, "Now you are one of us. You will not go back to Earth and show people the error of their ways!"

He threw his head back and laughed triumphantly. "People will continue to be selfish, greedy and cruel and we will always have power over them."

Trisa shuddered and took a step back, but the hooded figure took another step forward.

"Your Earth is doomed!" he shouted harshly.

The shocking truth of his words touched a chord within Trisa. She could not let this happen.

Wringing her hands nervously, she took a deep breath and mustered all the courage she had. Then, looking straight at him she said as bravely as she could, "I came here because I thought a little boy needed my help. But I was tricked. I will not let you or any evil creature destroy our Earth if I can help it."

The hooded man came forward aggressively. Terror gripped her, but she stood her ground.

And then he vanished.

---

72   Twisted

Trisa was left alone in the darkness, shivering in horror. Mejo had warned her about the deceptive Shadow Creatures who could change into any shape and form.

"And this one took the form of a lost child," murmured Trisa, terrified. Panic washed over her as she stared helplessly at the darkness ahead. How was she going to get back to the stairway?

She was about to turn back towards the light when a giggle, sharp, evil and eerie shot up through the gloom. Trisa was caught unawares. She gasped in shock as a thin shadowy image rose up to face her at the speed of light. Bulging eyes glinted darkly and a slow, malicious[73] grin spread across its nasty, hollow features.

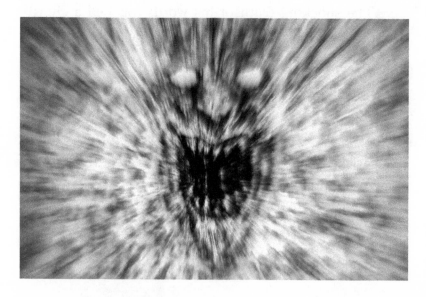

Bulging eyes glinted darkly

---

[73] Nasty

"Come," hissed the Shadow Creature. "Join us in the Pit of Gloom."

Trisa opened her mouth in a soundless scream.

"Join us, join us...," shrill voices chanted wickedly. In a flash, Trisa saw what looked like a giant cobweb being flung at her. Thin sharp knots tugged at her neck, arms and legs. She kicked and pushed, but she was securely tied in what felt like a fine, but extremely strong net. Within seconds, she was ensnared in it. She struggled to break free, but with every movement, the knots tightened painfully around her. She struggled in vain, screamed, and slipped over what felt like a dark precipice[74], falling at a tremendous speed, into a pit of nothingness.

"Join us, join us," shrill voices chanted wickedly

---

[74] Cliff

"Now you are one of us," she heard another harsh voice say, "trapped in this pit forever!"

"Help," she screamed, but her voice was muffled, drowned by the infinite vacuum. An unearthly chill stabbed her like a million knives, and she shivered uncontrollably. She could hear her own cries, distant and desperate, as she descended into the pit of darkness. The more she struggled, the more entangled she became in the invisible web, until finally, she could barely move.

"Add to the despair and the gloom," said a high-pitched voice with a wicked giggle.

"Sink in despair and stay locked in darkness like us," chanted another evil voice.

That's when Trisa remembered Mejo's words about the darkness.

The darkness doesn't last long, unless we want it to.

She closed her eyes tightly and concentrated on calming her mind. "The light does come eventually," she told herself. "As Mejo had said, we just got to wait for it."

Despite her situation, she felt herself start to relax slowly.

Do not stay focused on the dark moments.

Suddenly, strong hands grabbed at her and Trisa let out an involuntary scream.

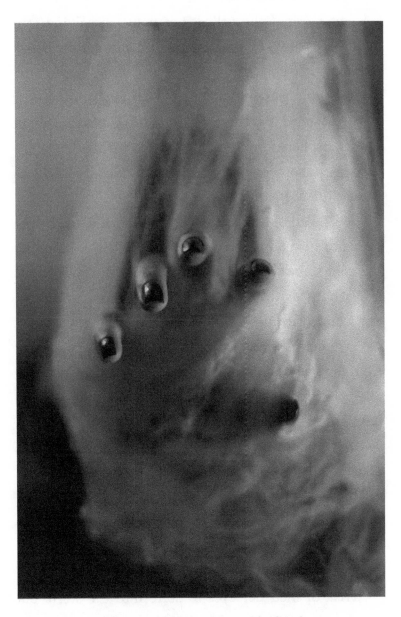

Suddenly, strong hands grabbed at her

Was this another monster?

"Let me go," she yelled, her panic dissolving into determination. "I will not let the darkness get the better of me. Let me go!"

She was released suddenly, and she felt herself falling at a great speed. But there was something different about the atmosphere now. It didn't seem so stifling[75].

"Please, someone help me," she shouted, as loudly as she could. "Mejo..."

She called out to him, feeling comforted just by the sound of his name. For a moment, she felt nothing but the cold stab of icy air. And then, she felt those hands again, but this time she thought she heard a voice too. She stopped struggling and strained her ears to listen.

"Trissaaaa...," She heard her name being called out from far away. Perhaps someone was trying to help her after all. She tried to respond, but something gripped her tightly.

"Let go of me!" yelled Trisa, kicking hard. But it was no use. She was held so tightly that now she simply could not move.

"Trisaaa...," she heard her name being called again. The voice sounded vaguely familiar, but Trisa could not place it.

"I got you!" said a deep voice, stern, but familiar. "Trisa!"

Trisa opened her eyes to stare into the stern, but deeply concerned face of Sister Pia.

---

[75] suffocating

HOME

For a horrifying second, Trisa wondered if Sister Pia was also trapped in this pit of darkness.

But then she felt the ground beneath her and the soft swathes of bed sheets that held her captive.

The comforting aroma of fresh coffee beans and hot cocoa wafted through.

And Trisa knew she was finally home.

She had no idea how she got there but her relief was so great, that she hugged Sister Pia.

Sister Pia gave a delighted little laugh and held her close.

"You've had a nightmare," she said softly, as she untangled the sheets gently. "What you need is a hot cup of cocoa."

"No!" exclaimed Trisa, suddenly wide awake and staring hard at Sister Pia. "He was here."

"Who?" asked Sister Pia shocked and visibly upset

"Who?" asked Sister Pia, shocked and visibly upset that a male individual may have entered the hallowed[76] living quarters of the religious.

"Who entered your room and where is he?" she demanded, straightening her skirt and grabbing the twelve inch wooden ruler from Trisa's desk, as she stood, ready to battle any intruder.

"Mejo," said Trisa softly. "The Storm Gatherer."

---

[76] Holy

"Oh you poor child," said Sister Pia, hastily discarding the ruler and putting her arm around Trisa. "The storm scared you and you dreamt about the old legend.

A hot cup of cocoa is all we need to set things right. I've made your favourite idlis[77] too."

She smiled and tucked a stray lock of hair behind Trisa's ear lovingly.

"Come along now. Get dressed and come into the kitchen for breakfast. Eat it while it's still steaming hot."

Sister Pia walked into the kitchen, leaving Trisa to dress up and follow.

Trisa stayed quiet as she folded her tangled bed sheets neatly.

"Certainly, this wasn't a dream," she thought to herself.

"He was right here."

She looked out of her window sadly. Will she ever see Mejo again?

---

[77] Rice cakes, a South Indian delicacy

A PLEASANT SURPRISE

T risa sighed, turned away from the window and shoved her hands into the pocket of her night shirt. Immediately, she gave a squeal of delight as she felt something soft and round. It was the strange, sweet berry that Mejo had plucked and given her while they were in the deep forest – the rare pink Karonda berry. One of them must have rolled off and fallen into her pocket as she sat on the branch.

The Karonda berry was the prettiest pink she had ever seen

She held it carefully in her hand and looked at it in the sunlight. It was the prettiest pink she had ever seen – the colour of a summer sunrise.

Her heart gave a little leap of joy.

"He's real, then!" she whispered to herself, her eyes sparkling with happiness. "He's real!"

She hurried into the bathroom to get ready for breakfast.

Turning on the faucet, she stared at herself in the bathroom mirror.

A stream of hot water filled the wash basin and she reached for her brush.

She looked up at the mirror again and gasped, her heart beating wildly.

Wisps of steam formed the image of Mejo

Wisps of steam floated lazily and settled in a uniform pattern to form the image of Mejo.

"I am Mejo," he said simply. "My name means many things. It also means water. Whenever you see water, you see me."

Trisa was too surprised to speak.

So Mejo continued, "We saved you from the Shadow Creatures. You were already falling into a trance[78], but the other Storm Gatherers and I, grabbed you and brought you home before you were lost forever."

Trisa swallowed, dumbfounded.

"I – I'm sorry," she stammered, "I disobeyed you..."

"And so you did," agreed Mejo.

But then he added with a smile, "But your motives were unselfish. You took a risk, hoping to help someone who you thought needed help."

"Yes," whispered Trisa, as she remembered the dark faces pleading for help.

"Kindness is a powerful and magical thing, Trisa," said Mejo softly. "It is a gift that all are blessed with, but that few choose to use – a heavenly boomerang that somehow finds its way back to you. Not everyone understands that."

Trisa listened intently, staring up at Mejo, quite delighted that he was real and not just a dream.

---

[78] A hypnotic state

Trisa stared up at Mejo in delight

"Once, every hundred years, the Storm Gatherers choose a kind and special soul. We help them unlock mental barriers of fear and other negative things, so that more kindness can fill that space."

He stared at her for a long moment. "This time the Storm Gatherers chose you."

"But that's not all," he continued, smiling his watery grin.

"Grandma wanted you to have this."

He opened his palm to reveal a strange object - small and shining, as if it was made of glass.

"You have kindness in your heart," said Mejo gently, "There's courage there too."

And then he added softly, "But it is your kindness that saved you."

He threw what looked like a small round ball of water at her, very much like a transparent tennis ball.

Only, it wasn't.

She caught it midair, and stared at it in wonder.

Lightning flashed within the ball

It felt like a light, crystal clear ball, filled with water. But trapped within it, was a sliver of what looked like lightning. It flashed periodically, lighting the ball with the soft colours of a rainbow.

"Keep it safe," said Mejo, as he slowly began to dissipate. "It is infused with magical powers that are activated only by acts of kindness. You will learn how to use it in time."

"Wait," said Trisa, but there was nothing left of Mejo, just stray wisps of steam.

A MOST
ENLIGHTENING
LESSON

Trisa dressed quickly and glanced out her bedroom
window at the garden below. Everything looked wet,
but clean. The storm was over and there was just a fine
mist of rain. Birds chirped happily and the air smelt of
the Earth - sweet and pure.

"Everything looks so radiant,' said Trisa

"Everything looks so radiant," said Trisa as she turned away and skipped down the hall and into the kitchen.

"Ah there you are," said Sister Pia as Trisa entered the kitchen, ready for breakfast. She stood by the large kitchen window, looking out at the flooded streets and a few broken branches. "Look at what the storm has done," she said.

"It's not the storm so much as us humans, Sister Pia," said Trisa softly.

"Ooohh???" asked Sister Pia questioningly, her eyes as big as saucers behind her black rimmed spectacles. "And how is that so, do tell me, young lady."

"Well," answered Trisa, clearing her throat. "When we litter, we cause drains to get clogged. And when we cut down trees we loosen the soil and that causes floods too."

Sister Pia stared at Trisa with her mouth open in the shape of a silent "O" of surprise.

"And here I thought you didn't like Geography and the study of Our Environment!"

"Oh, I love Geography, Sister Pia," laughed Trisa happily. "The storm taught me so much last night!"

"Hmmmm," said Sister Pia thoughtfully, with her hands on her hips.

Then she straightened her apron, shook her head and pointed to a dish of steaming Idlis. "Come along now and eat while the food is still hot."

And she added with a smile, "We will discuss this more in detail at our next Geography class. Perhaps you have a message for us on environment protection."

"I also have a nice message about enjoying the beauty of storms, and about the importance of being kind and compassionate." said Trisa. "Storms are certainly nothing to be afraid of."

"You are absolutely right, Trisa," said Sister Pia. "Now come along and dig in before those nice rice cakes get cold."

At breakfast, Trisa held her hot cup of cocoa close to her chest. So much had happened, and now she was no longer afraid of storms, or of the unknown.

She stared out of the large window across the kitchen table. A shimmering rainbow glowed in the distance. From where she sat at the kitchen table, everything seemed clean, fresh and new. Birds sang happily and leaves shone brilliantly in every shade of green.

Rice cakes (Idlis) and chutney

Trisa popped a piece of rice cake soaked in coconut and raisin chutney into her mouth. Delicious!

A new thought floated into her head and she smiled to herself.

"Every dark storm brings with it a new and brilliant light, turning nightmares into dream adventures. And that magical key to unlock our fears and overcome them lies deep within us all. We only need the courage to use it."

A MESSAGE FROM TRISA TO THE READER

Hey everyone, I hope you enjoyed my adventures in 'Storm Gatherers.'

Look out for more thrills and chills, magic and mystery coming up as I learn how to use the enchanted crystal ball that Mejo gave me.

Join me as the magic ball opens strange new worlds that we can explore together. There are long lost secrets and special treasures to be discovered.

But we need to be careful.

The crystal ball is powerful, rare and precious. It is the only one of its kind on Earth.

Evil shadow creatures are attracted to it and will try to steal it.

We must do all we can to protect it and ourselves from eternal doom.

I look forward to seeing you again, as I step out into a new adventure.

Trisa

ABOUT THE AUTHOR

Crystal Valladares is a prolific writer, poet and teacher. Her writings uncover a clear and tranquil flow of thought, the beauty of the English Language, and a deep insight into the magical world that attracts children and awakens their imagination. Storm Gatherers invites all children to explore this world.

NOTE

126

NOTE